Melody Mooner
Takes Lessons

Written by Frank B. Edwards
Illustrated by John Bianchi

The year that she turned 6, Melody Mooner said, "I want to take lessons. I want to be good at something special. But I don't know what."

In January, Mother Mooner took her skating, but Melody said, "I don't think so.

"I hate falling down on cold ice."

In February, Father Mooner sent her to ski school, but Melody said, "I don't think so.

"I could never go down hills so fast."

In March, Grandmother Mooner paid for ballet lessons, but Melody said, "I don't think so.
"All that twirling makes me dizzy."

In April, Grandfather Mooner signed her up for gymnastics, but Melody said, "I don't think so.
"I don't like to dangle."

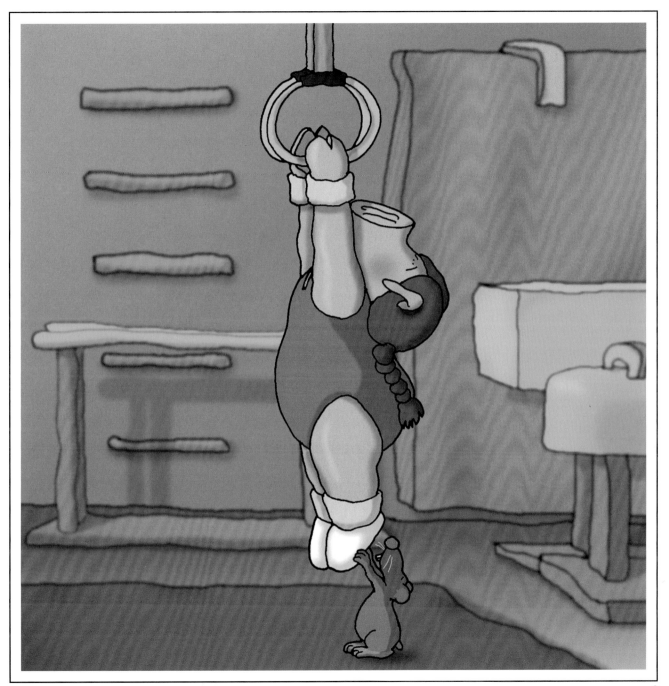

In May, Mortimer Mooner brought her to judo class, but Melody said, "I don't think so. "Everything seems to be upside down."

In June, the whole Mooner family took her to soccer practice, but Melody said, "I don't think so.
"I love the running, but I hate the kicking."

In July and August, Melody Mooner tried all kinds of lessons. She started painting . . . and swimming. She played tennis and baseball. She even took horseback-riding lessons. But each time, she said, "I don't think so.

"These things are all very interesting, but I want to learn something that is perfect for me."

In September, Melody went to her very first music recital. While Grandmother Mooner dreamed of the piano, Melody was fascinated by the horns — especially the tuba.

In October, Melody received a very special birthday present. It was a tuba, complete with music lessons.

In November, Melody practised every day until she could play one note perfectly.

And in December, Melody Mooner joined the Schnitzelville Junior Marching Band.

"Thank you for letting me try so many different things," she told her family after her first parade. "At last, I found the tuba."

And the rest of the Mooners smiled happily while they listened to Melody practise a new note . . .

. . . again and again and again.